The New Adventures of MARY-KATE & ASHLEY™

The Case Of The MISSING MUMMY™

The New Adventures of

MARY-KATE & ASHLEY™

The Case Of The MISSING MUMMY™

by Francess Lantz

DUALSTAR PUBLICATIONS  PARACHUTE PRESS

SCHOLASTIC INC.

New York Toronto London Auckland Sydney
Mexico City New Delhi Hong Kong

DUALSTAR PUBLICATIONS ™ PARACHUTE PRESS

Dualstar Publications
c/o Thorne and Company
1801 Century Park East
Los Angeles, CA 90067

Parachute Press
156 Fifth Avenue
Suite 325
New York, NY 10010

Published by Scholastic Inc.

With special thanks to Robert Thorne and Harold Weitzberg.

Printed in the U.S.A.
December 1998
ISBN: 0-590-29404-0
A B C D E F G H I J

1

MEETING THE MUMMY!

"I can't wait to see the mummy!" I said to my twin sister, Ashley. I slid into my seat on the school bus.

Ashley sat down next to me and grinned. "Me, too."

Our fifth-grade class was about to leave on a field trip. We were going to visit the Egyptian exhibit at our local museum. The Egyptian exhibit was closing next week, so this was our last chance to see it.

"I know why the Egyptian wing is closing,"

Patty O'Leary announced. She took a seat across the aisle from us.

"Why?" I asked.

"Because it's boring! Nobody wants to see it, so they're shutting it down."

"It is *not* boring," Peter Lopez said. He sat behind us. "The Egyptian wing is filled with all kinds of amazing stuff from ancient Egypt. Really *old* amazing stuff!"

"Name *one* amazing thing," Patty demanded.

"A real mummy!" Peter replied.

"*What*?" Patty cried. "I don't want to see a mummy! Mummies can put curses on people!"

"That's silly," Ashley said. "There's no such thing as a curse."

"I'm not so sure," our friend Tim Park said. "I've read about the King Tut mummy. At the entrance to his tomb, it says that anyone who enters will die."

"I don't believe it," I said. "That's just a superstition."

"Maybe it is just a superstition," Peter said.

"But a lot of people believe it's true."

"I don't care what anyone says," Patty insisted. "I'm not going anywhere near that mummy!" She flipped her brown ponytail over her shoulder, then stared out the window.

"Well, I think mummies are cool!" I said to Ashley.

"And mysterious!" Ashley replied.

I grinned. Ashley and I both love anything mysterious. That's because we're detectives. We run the Olsen and Olsen Mystery Agency out of the attic of our house in California.

"It's too bad Clue can't come with us today," I told Ashley.

Clue is our basset hound. She has a great nose for sniffing out evidence. So Ashley and I made her a silent partner in our detective agency.

"I don't think dogs are allowed on school buses," Ashley said, laughing.

That's Ashley—logical! Even though we're twins, we're totally different. Ashley is always

logical—she likes to think things through. I like to jump right into things!

Our friend Samantha Samuels boarded the bus. She tried to sit next to Patty. But Patty put her backpack on the seat beside her. That way, no one could sit next to her.

I glanced at Samantha and rolled my eyes. Sam shrugged and grinned. Her curly red hair bounced around her face, and her brown eyes were bright. She sat behind Patty.

Patty totally deserved the nickname we gave her: Princess Patty. She lives right next door to Ashley and me. Patty is the most spoiled, stuck-up girl in our whole school. Her parents give her whatever she wants—and she wants *everything*!

Our teacher, Mr. Weitzberg, climbed aboard and sat in the first row. He motioned to the driver, and the bus pulled away from the curb.

"Mr. Weitzberg," Tim called. He pushed his long black hair out of his eyes. "Will we get to see the dinosaur exhibit, too?"

“Not today,” Mr. Weitzberg replied. “I want to make sure you all see the Egyptian wing before it closes.”

“My older brother Bobby works there,” Peter told the class. “This is his last week, though. He won’t have a job after the wing closes. But he’s going to give our class a special tour.”

“That’s right,” Mr. Weitzberg said. “It’s going to be a very special tour. We’re going to have the museum all to ourselves this morning!”

I glanced out the window. The museum was right around the corner. I didn’t know it then—but our next mystery was right around the corner, too!

The Mummy Moved!

The bus pulled into the parking lot, and we all got out. A tall, dark-haired teenager with a cast on his arm came out of the building to meet us.

"You must be Bobby Lopez," Mr. Weitzberg said.

"That's me," he said, smiling. "Is everyone ready to meet the mummy?"

"Yes!" we all cheered—except Patty. She was too busy combing her hair.

"What happened to your arm?" Samantha

asked, as we walked toward the entrance.

"Skateboard wipe-out," he explained. "Broke my arm in two places!"

Bobby led us inside.

I looked around. Just a few lights were on. The exhibits were dark and deserted. The only sound we heard were our footsteps *tap*, *tap*, *tapping* on the marble floor.

"This is so cool!" I said to Ashley. My voice echoed back at me.

"Most of the things you'll see in the Egyptian wing are about three thousand years old," Bobby explained as we walked down the main hallway.

"Tell them about the mummy," Peter said.

"First," Bobby said, "let me tell you what a mummy *is*. In ancient Egypt, dead people were tightly wrapped in strips of cloth, then buried in a tomb. Their bodies could last forever that way," he explained.

"You mean there's a dead body right here in this museum?" Patty cried.

Bobby laughed. "Well, I guess you could say that."

Patty's mouth dropped open. Her eyes widened. "Well, *I'm* not going anywhere near it!"

"Is the mummy a king, like King Tut?" Tim asked.

"We don't know," Bobby said. "Actually, we don't know very much about our mummy at all. It was given to the museum years and years ago."

"Sounds mysterious!" I said.

"I agree," Bobby said. "But most people want to see *famous* mummies. That's why the Egyptian wing is closing. We just don't get enough visitors."

"Told you so, Peter," Patty said. "*Bor-ing*!"

Bobby smiled at Patty. "Well, there is *one* thing very special about our mummy," he said.

"What?" Patty asked.

"The curse!" Bobby answered.

3

CREEPY CURSE!

"See?" Patty cried to everyone. "I told you mummies can put curses on people!"

"Wait a minute, everybody," Ashley said. "Let's listen to what Bobby has to say about the curse—*then* we can argue. Bobby, can you tell us more about it?"

"Sure," Bobby said. "Let me show you something. Then you can decide if the mummy's curse is real."

Bobby led us past other exhibits to the entrance of the Egyptian wing. Above the

doorway to the mummy room was a carved turquoise beetle. Beneath the beetle was some ancient Egyptian writing.

"This is a scarab," Bobby explained, pointing to the beetle. "According to legend, the scarab was found on the entrance to this mummy's tomb."

"What does the writing say, Bobby?" Ashley asked.

"It says: 'Whoever touches this scarab will wake the mummy and be cursed!'" Bobby told us.

Patty shrieked and jumped back.

"I'm not scared," I said. I reached up and touched the scarab.

"Me, either," Ashley said. She touched it, too.

Peter hesitated. Then he brushed his fingers across the scarab.

Soon every kid in the class was crowding around to touch the scarab. Everyone except Princess Patty.

"No way I'm touching that! " Patty said. "I'm not going to wake the mummy. I don't want a curse put on me."

"Let's go inside," Bobby said.

We all followed Bobby—except Patty and Mr. Weitzberg. Patty stayed just outside the mummy room, watching us. And Mr. Weitzberg left to talk to the director of the museum.

"Cool!" I said when I entered the room. It was decorated to look exactly like an Egyptian tomb. It had a curved ceiling and a dirt floor. And pictures of people and animals were painted right on the walls!

A huge stone coffin lay in the center of the room. Bobby told us that the coffin is called a sarcophagus.

"The mummy must be in there." Ashley pointed to the coffin.

Wow! I couldn't believe it. In just a few seconds, I would see a real mummy!

Everyone made a circle around the coffin.

"How weird!" Bobby said. "The sarcopha-

gus is closed!" He stared at the coffin.

"Why is that weird?" Ashley asked.

"The lid is always open so people can look at the mummy," Bobby explained.

"Why is it closed, then?" Peter asked.

"I don't know," Bobby said, frowning. He walked over to the sarcophagus and grabbed one end of the lid. "Can someone help me move this? I can't do it with my broken arm."

"We will," I said. As Ashley and I helped Bobby shove the lid aside, my heart began to pound. I had never seen a mummy before. I was excited—but a little scared at the same time.

When the lid was off, I looked inside—and gasped!

"It's empty!" I cried as I stared inside. "The mummy is missing!"

Patty poked her head into the room and let out a scream.

"Maybe the mummy is alive," Peter said in a worried whisper. "Maybe it's walking around

the museum somewhere!"

"Of course it's alive!" Patty shrieked. "You all touched the scarab. You woke it up! And now you're all cursed!"

"Patty," Ashley said, "we touched the scarab about thirty seconds ago!"

"So?" Patty asked.

"So," I explained, "even if the curse *is* real—which it *isn't*—how could the mummy get out of its coffin and walk away without our seeing it?"

"*You're* the detective, Mary-Kate—*you* tell *us*," Patty snapped.

I thought for a second. "I know!" I said. "Somebody *moved* the mummy."

"I'm sure Mary-Kate is right, Patty," Ashley agreed.

"It has to be here somewhere," I said.

"Bobby, Mary-Kate and I are detectives. Would it be okay if we searched the museum for the mummy?" Ashley asked.

"I guess so," he said. "As long as you're very

careful. I'll have to wait here with the rest of your class until your teacher comes back."

Ashley and I took off.

This was more exciting than ever.

The mummy was missing—and we'd found our next big case!

4

The Search Begins

"Okay," Ashley said. "Let's start here—in the insect room." She pulled her detective notebook out of her backpack. Ashley likes to write things down: lists of clues, lists of possible suspects, lists of *everything*!

We stepped into the dark room.

Bzzz. Bzzz. Bzzz. I heard the sound of thousands of buzzing bees. They flew around in a glass-covered honeycomb as part of an exhibit. All those bees were giving me the creeps!

I searched around, but I didn't see the mummy.

"Let's try the dinosaur exhibit," Ashley suggested.

We hurried down the hall and walked into the huge dinosaur exhibit.

A flying pterodactyl was hanging right over my head! The wings were so huge! I could imagine it swooping down and—

"Come on, Mary-Kate!" Ashley said. "Stop staring at the dinosaur and start looking for the mummy."

Oops! Ashley was right. I checked out the room, but there was no mummy anywhere.

"Where could it be?" I asked.

"It has to be here somewhere," Ashley replied.

"It *has* to be," I agreed. "Patty is wrong. There's no way the mummy woke up and walked off."

"Patty is *definitely* wrong," Ashley said. "Let's check out that room up ahead."

We raced into the next room. “Wow!” A huge stegosaurus and a triceratops towered over me. “These are amazing!”

“I know, Mary-Kate,” Ashley said. “But we can’t stop to look at them. We have to find that mummy!”

We hurried through the doorway into another room, and another room after that.

We saw lots and lots of dinosaurs—but still no mummy!

“Where is that mummy?” I wondered out loud.

“I don’t know,” Ashley said. “But it has to be here someplace!”

There was one more room in the dinosaur wing left to search.

We walked inside.

It was the darkest room of all. No lights were on. There were no windows for the sun to stream in.

In the center of the room stood a Tyrannosaurus rex—the tallest, meanest–

looking dinosaur I'd ever seen!

And next to the dinosaur stood something even scarier.

The mummy!

5

THE CASE GETS WEIRDER!

"Whoa!" I was finally staring at a real live mummy!

It was short. Not much taller than Ashley and I—and we're only ten years old. People must have been much shorter back in the mummy's days, I thought.

The mummy was wrapped in a lot of brownish-yellow linen. *What did the person inside look like*? I wondered. Then I realized I didn't want to know!

"How do you think the mummy got here?" I

asked Ashley. I stared at the mummy.

"I don't have a clue," Ashley said. "But that's what we have to find out!"

"Let's go tell Bobby and everyone that we found it," I said.

We raced back to the main lobby. Mr. Weitzberg, Bobby, and our class stood near the front door of the museum. "I told your teacher what happened," Bobby said. "Did you two find the mummy?"

"Yes!" I told him. "It's leaning against the Tyrannosaurus rex!"

"But that's impossible!" Bobby exclaimed.

"What's impossible, Bobby?" a woman's voice asked.

We all turned around to see a tall, thin woman coming toward us. She had short blond hair, and she was wearing big red-rimmed glasses.

"Hi, Ms. Pemberly," Bobby said. "These are the kids from my brother Peter's fifth-grade class. Kids, this is Ms. Pemberly, the director

of the museum."

"Someone moved the mummy," I explained to Ms. Pemberly. "My sister and I found it in the dinosaur wing."

"But that's impossible!" Ms. Pemberly said.

"But it's true," Ashley replied. "We'll show you!"

Everyone followed Ashley and me into the dinosaur wing.

"Ewwwwwwww!" Patty cried, covering her eyes with one hand. "I'm not looking at that creepy thing!"

"Ms. Pemberly," Ashley said, "why is it impossible that someone moved the mummy?"

"Because it was in its sarcophagus last night," she explained. "I saw it myself right before I locked up the museum and left."

"Maybe someone broke in last night—or early this morning," I said.

Ms. Pemberly shook her head. "No chance of that. If anyone tried to enter the museum through the doors or windows, an alarm

would have gone off."

Ashley sighed. "So there's no way anyone can break into the museum?"

"Not unless they know the alarm system's password—and I'm the only one who does," Ms. Pemberly said. "The system is foolproof."

"Can you think of any explanation for how the mummy ended up in the dinosaur wing?" Ashley asked.

"None!" Ms. Pemberly said. "I'm stumped!"

And so were we!

6

THE CURSE GETS WORSE!

"I think Patty is right," Peter said on the bus ride back to school. "We woke up the mummy—and it walked away."

"Come on, Peter," I said. "You don't really believe that."

"Okay, Miss-Know-It-All!" Patty said to me. "*You* explain how the mummy got into the dinosaur exhibit!"

"I don't know—*yet*," I snapped. "But I know mummies can't walk around by themselves!"

"Yes, they can!" Patty yelled. "One just did!"

Was Patty right? I didn't think so.

"All I know is that it was nice of Ms. Pemberly to let us visit the dinosaur exhibit," Tim said to me.

"I guess she felt bad about what happened in the Egyptian wing," I said.

We got to spend a whole hour checking out the dinosaurs! But when I saw the Tyrannosaurus rex, all I could think about was the mummy. How had it gotten there?

The bus pulled up to our school, and we all got out. Everyone was buzzing about the moving mummy as we headed to the cafeteria for lunch.

"Okay, kids," Mr. Weitzberg said after we ate. "It's time to get started on our painting for the school art contest. Let's head over to the art room."

Cool! I thought. Every class in the school was creating a painting. The theme was school spirit. The principal was going to pick the winner and display the art in the main hall all year.

Ms. Clark, the art teacher, waited for us in the art room. "Hi, everyone!" she said, smiling. "Head over to your cubbies and put on your painting smocks. It's time to start painting!"

I made a beeline for my cubby. But it was empty. My smock was missing!

I turned to Ashley. "Is my smock in your cubby?"

"No," she said, frowning. "And mine isn't in my cubby either."

"Hey! My smock is missing, too," Samantha announced.

"Mine, too," a few other kids called out.

"Ms. Clark," I called, "all our smocks are missing!"

"Everyone's smocks? Missing? How strange!" she said.

"Mine is right here where I left it," Patty said. She held up her smock and waved it around.

"Maybe someone moved our smocks," Ashley said.

"Ha!" Patty said. "Just like someone moved the mummy?"

I ignored Patty. "Can't we borrow smocks from another class, Ms. Clark?"

"I'm really sorry, kids," the art teacher said, "but all the classes will be working on their art projects today. Their smocks need to be clean and dry for them to use."

Everyone groaned.

"I'll tell you what," Ms. Clark said, "if I find your smocks, you can come back tomorrow and have extra time to work on your painting."

"Thanks, Ms. Clark," Ashley said.

"It's the mummy's curse," Peter said on the way back to our classroom.

I made a face. "Not that curse thing again!"

"Think about it," Peter said. "Patty is the *only one* of us who didn't touch the scarab. And Patty's smock is the *only one* that isn't missing."

The kids nodded in agreement. "Peter's right," someone said.

"It's all your fault, Mary-Kate and Ashley," Patty said. "You didn't believe in the curse. Then you touched the scarab. You're the ones who made the mummy mad."

"Thanks to you, we can't start our painting," Peter griped.

"Don't blame Mary-Kate and Ashley," Samantha said. "We all touched the scarab."

"That's true," Tim agreed.

"Yes," Patty agreed, "but they touched it *first.*"

"Yeah," I heard someone murmur. "It's their fault."

I felt awful! I glanced at Ashley and saw that she did, too. Practically everyone we knew was mad at us. That was worse than having a mummy mad at us!

But I wasn't about to give in. Not when I knew we were right.

"Just you wait," I said. "That curse isn't real—and Ashley and I are going to prove it!"

We all walked into our classroom.

"Mary-Kate," Ashley said as we sat down, "this case is getting weirder and weirder. Now we have *two* cases to solve!"

"What do you mean?" I asked.

"The mummy moving is one mystery. And the missing smocks is another!" she said.

"Well, I know who hid our smocks!" I declared.

"Who?" Ashley asked.

"Princess Patty! She wants to prove she's right—that the mummy cursed us. So she hid our smocks."

"Maybe," Ashley said. "But we don't know that for sure. We have a lot more investigating to do."

If Ashley was right—if Patty didn't steal our smocks—then who did?

The only other person I could think of right now was—the mummy!

Was Patty right?

Did the mummy really put a curse on us?

7

A Scary Surprise

"The mummy moved again last night!" Peter yelled. He and Patty ran up to us in the school yard the next morning.

"How do you know?" I asked.

"Ms. Pemberly called Bobby this morning to tell him," he explained. "She found the mummy leaning against her desk in her office!"

"Do you believe me now?" Patty demanded. "The mummy is walking around everywhere!"

"No, I don't!" I said as we headed indoors.

Well, maybe I wasn't so sure if I believed her or not. But I would never tell Patty that!

"Ms. Pemberly called the newspaper," Peter went on. "A reporter is coming to the museum today to do a story on the moving mummy."

"Let's go to the museum after school today," I said to Ashley as we took our seats. "We can search for clues."

Mr. Weitzberg came into the classroom. "I have some bad news for you," he said. "Your art smocks haven't been found. Tomorrow, bring in an old shirt that you can use as a smock. Now, let's get out our science books and turn to page fifty-four."

I reached into my desk for my science book. But instead of a textbook, I felt something slippery in there.

Something long and slippery.

And whatever it was, it was moving!

I looked inside—and screamed!

Slithering inside my desk was a big, black snake!

I jerked back so fast, I knocked my chair over.

Then I realized someone else was screaming. It was Ashley.

A snake was sliding out of her desk, too!

"Snakes!" we both yelled.

Mr. Weitzberg ran down the aisle and grabbed the snakes. "Garter snakes. Completely harmless," he said. Then he dropped the snakes out the window.

"I want to know who put those snakes in Mary-Kate and Ashley's desks," he demanded.

"It's the mummy's curse!" Patty cried.

Peter nodded. "My brother told me the curse is twice as bad on people who don't believe in it."

"That's why Mary-Kate and Ashley are the only ones with snakes in their desks," Patty said.

"I don't want to hear another word about the mummy's curse," Mr. Weitzberg said. "Now who did this?"

When no one confessed, Mr. Weitzberg looked very upset. "I don't know who did this, but I want this mischief to stop now. Do you all understand me?"

Everyone nodded.

"Fine," Mr. Weitzberg said. "Now, open your science books to page fifty-four and answer the questions at the bottom of the page."

The class got to work. The room was so quiet, I could hear my pencil scratching against the paper.

I glanced over at Patty. She looked up and shot me a smug little smile.

"You're cursed!" she whispered to me.

The minute the final bell rang, Ashley and I raced outside to our bikes.

"Let's pick up Clue, then head straight to the museum," Ashley said.

"Ashley, do you think the same person who hid our smocks put the snakes in our desks?" I asked her.

"I don't know," she said, pedaling hard. "But it's starting to look as if someone really wants us to think our class is cursed."

"Well, I'll bet that someone is Patty," I said. "She'll do anything to prove she's right about the mummy's curse."

"Maybe," Ashley said. "But do you really think Patty would touch a snake? *Two* snakes?"

"You have a point," I said. "But I still think it's her."

"It might be," Ashley said. "But we don't know that for sure."

"It has to be Patty," I insisted. "Because if it's not, then it has to be..." I didn't finish my sentence.

"Who?" Ashley asked, glancing at me.

"The mummy!" I said. "I mean, do you think it's possible? Do you think the mummy really could have put a curse on our class?"

"No way!" Ashley said, as we turned down our street. "If it's not Patty, then it's someone

else. But it's definitely not the mummy."

"Then who?" I asked as we pedaled into our driveway.

"I don't know," Ashley said as we headed inside. "That's what we have to find out."

After a snack of milk and cookies, Ashley, Clue, and I set off for the museum.

By the time we got there, the lobby was packed with reporters and people carrying video cameras.

"I thought *one* reporter was coming," I said.

"It looks as if Ms. Pemberly called every newspaper, radio station, and TV station in California!" Ashley said.

I saw Ms. Pemberly step out of her office. All the reporters and cameramen crowded around her.

"Is it true?" one of the reporters asked. "Is the museum's mummy really walking around?"

"Well," Ms. Pemberly said with a big smile, "the mummy *has* been found in different parts of the museum."

"Like where?" another reporter shouted out.

"Yesterday," Ms. Pemberly said, "a group of schoolchildren found it in the dinosaur wing. And this morning, I discovered the mummy in my office. It was leaning against my desk! It's quite a mystery!"

Ashley took out her notebook and wrote down the information Ms. Pemberly gave.

Ms. Pemberly turned and smiled into the cameras. "I invite the public to come visit the museum. Who knows? You just might see the mummy move."

I turned to Ashley. "By tomorrow, the Egyptian wing is going to be packed with people wanting to see the mummy," I said.

"Ms. Pemberly must be really happy about that," Ashley said. "She was going to shut down the wing because no one was coming to see it."

"And now," I said, "everyone will want to check it out."

"Mary-Kate!" Ashley said. "That gives Ms. Pemberly a motive for moving the mummy!"

"You're right!" I said. "To get more visitors to the museum. Do you think she's guilty?"

"I don't know," Ashley said. "But we need to find out! She *is* the only one who knows the password to the alarm system."

She turned to the *SUSPECTS* page of her notebook. She wrote down Ms. Pemberly's name.

I felt a tap on my shoulder. It was Bobby Lopez.

"Hi, Bobby," I said. "Sounds as if the Egyptian wing is going to get a ton of visitors now!"

"I know! Isn't it great?" he said, reaching down to pet Clue on the head. "Maybe Ms. Pemberly won't have to close the exhibit after all."

"Bobby," Ashley asked, "have you noticed anything unusual in the Egyptian wing lately? Has anything been taken or moved—other

than the mummy, that is?"

"I don't think so," he said. "It's too bad Joe Marshall doesn't work in the museum anymore. He was a great night watchman. If a dust ball moved during his watch, he could tell you!"

"The museum used to have a night watchman?" I asked.

Bobby nodded. "Ms. Pemberly fired Joe a few weeks ago—after the new alarm system was put in. She said he wasn't needed anymore. He's still really upset about losing his job."

Upset enough to break in and move the mummy? I wondered.

Did he want to prove to Ms. Pemberly that she still needed a night watchman?

Maybe!

And that meant we now had mummy mover suspect #2!

8

ONE MAD MUMMY MOVER?

It was time to talk to Joe Marshall. Bobby told us Mr. Marshall lived at 52 Greenleaf Street. That was right behind the museum.

Ashley, Clue, and I climbed the steps to his house. I rang the bell.

A big man with a bushy mustache opened the door. "If you're selling candy or magazines, I don't want any!" he snapped.

"We're not selling anything," I said. "I'm Mary-Kate Olsen, and this is my sister, Ashley. This is Clue, our dog."

"We're detectives investigating the moving mummy at the museum," Ashley explained. "We were wondering if we could ask you a few questions about the museum—if you're Joe Marshall?"

"That's me," he said. "Aren't you two kind of young to be detectives?"

"No," I told him. "We solve mysteries all the time."

"That's cute." He smiled.

I could tell he didn't really believe we were detectives, but he agreed to answer our questions anyway.

"You used to be the museum's night watchman, right?" I asked.

"That's right," he said. "I worked there for almost fourteen years!" His face turned red. "Then they put in that stupid alarm system and fired me!"

Stupid alarm system? I thought. Mr. Marshall *is* very upset!

"Ms. Pemberly says the alarm system is

foolproof," Ashley pointed out.

"Ha!" he said. "How foolproof could it be if someone is breaking in and moving that creepy mummy around! I'll bet Ms. Pemberly is sorry she fired me now!"

"But the alarm system has a password that only Ms. Pemberly knows. Are you sure that someone could crack the password and get in?" Ashley asked.

"I doubt the mummy is walking around by itself, girls," he said.

"Do you have any idea who might be breaking in?" I asked.

"Not a clue, girls. But I wouldn't be surprised if Ms. Pemberly begs me to take my old job back soon. That alarm system is obviously worthless!"

"Just one more question—" I began.

"There's my phone," Mr. Marshall cut me off. "Got to go, girls," he said. Then he closed the door.

"Ashley," I said, "Mr. Marshall is definitely

a suspect now!"

"I agree," she said, getting out her detective notebook. She wrote down his name under *SUSPECTS*. "He wants to prove that someone can break into the museum. That way, he'll get his job back."

"So that makes two mummy mover suspects: Ms. Pemberly and Mr. Marshall. And one suspect for the mean tricks at school," I added. "Patty."

"We need to go home and think about all this," Ashley said. "And think hard—if we're ever going to solve this case!"

After dinner, Ashley and I headed up to our attic office. Clue padded after us.

"Okay, Mary-Kate," Ashley said. "Let's talk about what we know."

"Okay," I said. "First—the mummy."

"Someone is moving the mummy. Someone moved it two nights in a row."

"Right," I said. "Then there's the bad stuff

happening to our class. First, our smocks were stolen. And then we found those snakes in our desks!"

"Maybe the same person is moving the mummy and then making bad things happen to our class," Ashley said.

"Ms. Pemberly and Mr. Marshall both have strong motives for moving the mummy," I said. "But why would either of them do mean things to our class? Why would they want us to think the mummy cursed us?"

"Good question," Ashley said. "What would be the point? What happens in our class wouldn't help Ms. Pemberly get more visitors to the museum. And it wouldn't help Mr. Marshall get his job back."

"So we're right where we started. We have two separate mysteries to solve," I said.

"If only we could catch the mummy mover in the act of moving the mummy. That would solve one mystery!"

"Ashley!" I cried. "That's it!"

"What's it?" she asked.

"There's only one way to catch a mummy mover in the act!" I exclaimed.

Ashley grinned. "Stakeout!"

"Right!" I said. "Just you, me, Clue…and the mummy!"

9

Slumber Party with a Mummy

We ran downstairs and told our parents that we wanted to go on a stakeout at the museum. After we told them about the case, our dad called Ms. Pemberly.

An hour later, Ashley, Clue, and I stood outside the museum with our backpacks. I rang the buzzer.

Ms. Pemberly opened the door. "Hi, girls," she said, petting Clue's ear. "Come on in."

"Thanks for letting us have a stakeout, Ms. Pemberly," I said.

"No, thank *you*!" she said, smiling. "I can't wait to tell the reporters that the famous Trenchcoat Twins are staking out the museum to watch the mummy move!"

"Well…to watch the mummy *mover* move," Ashley said.

"We'll see, won't we!" Ms. Pemberly replied. "Well, you know the way to the Egyptian wing. Make yourselves comfortable. I have tons of paperwork to catch up on, so I'll be in my office if you need me."

"Thanks again, Ms. Pemberly," I said.

"Just be very careful, girls," Ms. Pemberly warned. "Your dad will be here at ten o'clock to pick you up. That gives you three hours to catch the mummy moving!"

We watched her walk down the hall to her office. She closed the door behind her.

Ashley, Clue, and I headed toward the Egyptian wing. The museum was even darker and quieter than when we were here with our class.

We walked past suits of armor and statues in antique costumes. I glanced into the dinosaur wing. In the dim light, the flying pterodactyl looked like a big, hungry monster.

Finally, we came to the mummy room. It was pitch dark except for a single spotlight that shone down on the open sarcophagus.

I paused at the entrance. "This is spookier than I thought it would be," I said.

"I know what you mean," Ashley replied. "Come on, let's go inside."

We walked into the mummy room and stepped up to the sarcophagus. "The mummy is right where it's supposed to be," Ashley said.

I stared down at the mummy. It looked mysterious and ghostly. "It looks almost alive," I whispered. "As if it could sit up and talk to us."

"Well, we won't have to worry about that," Ashley said with a grin. "I don't think it'll talk to us. It's mad at us, remember?"

Ashley and I sat down on the floor beside the sarcophagus. Clue sniffed around the room.

“Find anything suspicious, Clue?” I asked.

Clue wagged her tail. Then she plopped down next to me and closed her eyes.

“Some detective!” I said. “We haven’t been here ten minutes and she’s already asleep.”

“It must be nice being a dog,” Ashley said. “I couldn’t fall asleep in here even if I wanted to. It’s just too creepy sleeping in the same room with a mummy!”

“I agree,” I said. “It’s a good thing I brought these library books about mummies.” I pulled some out of my backpack. “That’ll keep us busy while we wait for the mummy mover.”

“[illegible]” Ashley said. “I just thought of something. We can’t even be sure the mummy mover—whoever it is—is going to move the mummy *tonight*.”

“But the mummy moved the last two nights in a row,” I replied. “So it probably will move

again tonight."

"That's a good point," Ashley said.

"I'll bet the mummy mover is Ms. Pemberly," I told Ashley. "She'll probably try to move the mummy tonight after we've left—or even while we're still here! Maybe she's planning to trick us into leaving the room for a few minutes, and then—"

"Mary-Kate!" Ashley interrupted me. "You just made me think of something. We forgot about another suspect!"

"Huh?" I asked. "Who?"

"Bobby Lopez!" Ashley said. "Don't you remember what Peter told us? That Bobby is going to lose his job because the Egyptian wing is closing. He has a motive, too—to get more visitors so he can keep his job."

"Right!" I said. "So now we have three mummy mover suspects: Ms. Pemberly, Mr. Marshall, and Bobby."

Or did we have *four* suspects...including the mummy? I wondered, staring at the coffin.

Ashley took her notebook out of her backpack. I watched her add Bobby Lopez's name to the list of suspects.

"Oh, no—it can't be Bobby," Ashley said. She erased his name. "He has a broken arm. There's no way he could lift the mummy with one hand."

"So we're back to Ms. Pemberly or Mr. Marshall," I said.

"I guess we should just wait for the mummy mover to strike," Ashley said. "Then we'll have all the clues, evidence, and proof we need!"

I nodded. We each reached for a book about mummies, switched on our flashlights, and started reading.

I learned lots of amazing things. I learned that some mummies have up to twenty layers of bandages wrapped around them. And that some mummies were buried with all their treasures—their gold, their paintings, and all their jewelry. That way, they believed, their valuable things would stay with them forever!

All of the sudden, there was a weird, creepy noise.

Thumpety-thump! Thumpety-thump!

Clue's eyes opened, and her ears shot up. Ashley looked up from her book.

Thumpety-thump! *Thumpety-thump*!

We heard a thumping sound, but we didn't know where it was coming from.

Thumpety-thump! *Thumpety-thump*!

But it was getting closer.

Thumpety-thump!

And closer.

Thumpety-thump! Thumpety-thump!

"What is *that*?" I shrieked.

10

THE STAKEOUT STRIKEOUT!

Thumpety-thump! Thumpety-thump!

Clue jumped to her feet and barked.

"Quiet, Clue!" I said.

I listened hard. "Ashley, those thumps sound as if they're coming from *inside* the walls!"

"How could someone be walking *inside* the walls?" Ashley asked.

Thumpety-thump! Thumpety-thump!

"I don't know," I said. "But the thumps are getting quieter now—as if they're moving

away from us. Whoever it is must have heard Clue barking!"

"Come on!" Ashley cried. "He's getting away! Let's follow the sound!"

We dashed out of the Egyptian wing with Clue at our heels.

We followed the sound to the other end of the museum. Then the thumps stopped.

We walked all around the museum, listening hard. But the sound was gone.

Ashley pressed her ear against the wall.

"I hear something!" she cried. "More thumps! But they're really faint. I can't tell where they're coming from—or where they're going!"

Clue cocked her head to one side. She let out a sharp bark, then turned and ran down the hallway.

"Follow her!" Ashley cried.

We took off after Clue.

"She's heading back to the Egyptian wing!" I said.

"Clue!" Ashley called. "Wait for us!"

We caught up with Clue in the mummy room. She stood next to the sarcophagus, barking wildly.

"What is it, Clue?" Ashley asked as we hurried over.

I looked into the sarcophagus—and my jaw dropped!

The coffin was empty!

The mummy was gone!

"I can't believe it!" Ashley cried.

"Let's go find Ms. Pemberly!" I said.

We raced to Ms. Pemberly's office and knocked on the door.

No answer.

"Ms. Pemberly!" Ashley cried. "Are you in there?"

"She *is* the mummy mover!" I said. "She's not in there!"

Then the door opened. Ms. Pemberly rubbed her eyes and put on her glasses. She yawned. "Mary-Kate, Ashley, what's wrong?"

Ashley and I looked at each other—and then we both gulped.

Ms. Pemberly couldn't have moved the mummy. She was sleeping! At least it looked like she was.

If she *was* asleep, that meant someone *had* broken into the museum. And that someone was probably still here!

"Ms. Pemberly," Ashley cried, "didn't you hear all the thumping noises? And Clue barking? The mummy is gone! We have to find it—and whoever moved it! Come on!"

"No, girls. We're not going anywhere," Ms. Pemberly said. "I'm calling your parents right now to come pick you up. I don't know what's going on here, but it's too dangerous for you to stay. After I call your parents, I'm calling the police."

Ms. Pemberly reached for the phone and started dialing.

"I don't get it," Ashley said with a sigh. "If the alarm didn't go off..."

"Then that leaves only one possibility," I said. "The mummy mover is coming in and out of the museum some other way."

"You're right," Ashley said. "That sound was coming from inside the walls. There has to be a way in from the outside that even Joe Marshall doesn't know about!"

"Or that he *does* know about," I said. "Because he's probably the mummy mover!"

"Let's investigate the outside of the building tomorrow after school," Ashley said. "Uh-oh!" she groaned.

"What's wrong?" I asked.

"School! Tomorrow! Every time the mummy moves," she said, "something bad happens to our class. I wonder what it will be this time!"

11

Bun-Bun Disappears!

"Come on, Mary-Kate!" Ashley said. "Pedal faster! We're going to be late for school!"

That's what I was trying to do—be late. The later I got to school, the later I'd find out if something horrible had happened to our class!

Ms. Pemberly called us that morning. She told us she'd found the mummy in the insect room. She also told us she and the police checked all the doors and windows—there

was no sign of a break-in.

"Well," I said to Ashley as we walked into school, "let's find out what happened this time."

In our classroom, we saw everyone crowded around the cages where our class rabbit and guinea pig are kept.

We walked closer. Fuzzball, the guinea pig, was in her cage. But Bun-Bun's cage...

It was empty!

Samantha had tears in her eyes. "I came in early to feed Bun-Bun, but he was missing."

"Maybe someone left the cage unlocked, and he got out," Ashley suggested.

Samantha shook her head. "I locked the cage myself yesterday afternoon. He's disappeared!"

Patty turned to me and Ashley. "I told you to stay away from that scarab," she said. "The mummy must be really mad! I bet Fuzzball will be next to disappear!"

"What are we going to do?" Peter asked

with a worried frown.

"We're going to sit down and open our math workbooks," Mr. Weitzberg said. "I've told the principal about Bun-Bun's disappearance. That's the best we can do for now. Did everyone remember to bring smocks today?"

"Yes," we all said.

"I didn't have to bring one," Patty said. "*Mine* wasn't missing." She glared at me.

"After recess, we'll get started on our class painting," Mr. Weitzberg said.

We all trudged slowly to our desks. We opened our workbooks, but no one was writing. Everyone kept glancing back at Bun-Bun's cage.

Out of the corner of my eye, I saw something moving. Was it Bun-Bun?

I spun my head around. No. It was only Patty scratching her arms.

Wait a minute! Patty was *scratching* her arms!

I leaned over and nudged Ashley. "Look," I

whispered. "I think we found our bunny snatcher."

"What do you mean?" Ashley whispered back.

"Mary-Kate and Ashley," Mr. Weitzberg called out. "Quiet."

"Let's talk at recess," I said.

When the bell rang, Ashley and I raced outside. We hid behind the big oak tree and spied on Patty. She sat on a swing and scratched her neck. Then her face. Then her arms. Then her neck again.

"Everyone knows Patty is allergic to small furry animals! She must have taken Bun-Bun!" I said.

"Maybe," Ashley said. "But Patty didn't know the mummy moved last night. So how would she know to do another mean thing today?"

"Oh. You're right," I said, frowning. "But maybe she did find out somehow that the mummy moved. Or maybe she just figured it

would move."

"No matter what," Ashley said, "we need proof."

"Patty scratching herself *is* proof!" I said. "If she didn't take Bun-Bun, why is she so itchy?"

"We need *real* proof," Ashley said.

Ashley always wants proof! But this time, I knew how to get it!

"Okay," I said. "Before we go back to the museum this afternoon, let's spy on Patty some more. I bet she'll lead us right to Bun-Bun!"

When school ended, Patty's mother picked her up in her fancy red sports car. We followed on our bikes.

We hid behind a tree until Patty went inside their huge ranch-style house. Then we crawled into the bushes under her open bedroom window.

I lifted my head and peeked into Patty's

room. She was talking on her purple telephone.

"Don't tell anyone I'm hiding him in my room," Patty said into the phone. Then she listened to the other person. "Of course I'm feeding him," she replied. "I'm giving him lots of lettuce."

"Aha!" I whispered to Ashley as I ducked back down. "She has to be talking about Bun-Bun!"

"It does sound that way," Ashley agreed.

"Thanks for helping me get him," Patty said. "You're my favorite cousin!"

I lifted my head again and peered into Patty's room. She hung up the telephone and walked over to her closet. Then she took out a cardboard box with holes in the top and set it on her purple-and white-striped bedspread.

She opened the box and sat down beside it. "Don't worry," I heard her say. "Tomorrow I'm going to buy you a nice new cage."

"Ashley!" I cried. "There's your proof!"

Ashley popped her head up to look.

And Patty chose that exact moment to stare out her window!

"Hey!" Patty shrieked. "What are you two doing out there?" She marched over to the window.

"You stole Bun-Bun!" I said. "You have him in that box."

"Some detective you are, Mary-Kate Olsen!" Patty snapped. "You can't even tell the difference between a rabbit and a hamster!"

Huh?

"That's not Bun-Bun in there," Patty said. "That's my brand-new purebred hamster, Queenie."

"But you're allergic to hamsters," I said.

"*So*?" Patty snapped. "I wanted one. Everyone else gets to have a pet—except me! I saved my allowance and bought Queenie with my own money. My parents would flip if they knew I had a hamster in my room!"

Patty lifted her new hamster out of the box

and scratched its furry head. "Now do you believe me?"

Boy, was I embarrassed! "I'm sorry, Patty," I said. "I was wrong." I tried to reach in through the window to pet Queenie.

"You should be sorry!" Patty said. "Sorry for waking up the mummy!" She snatched the hamster away and put it back into the box. Then she marched over to the window and slammed it shut!

12

THE SECRET TUNNEL!

Ashley and I hopped onto our bikes and headed to the museum. No one was around. I checked my watch. It was six-thirty. The museum was closed for the day.

"I can't believe Patty is innocent!" I said. "I was sure she was the one playing the mean tricks on our class."

"That's why I tell you not to jump to conclusions," Ashley said. "We must be missing something. There has to be something we haven't thought of."

But *what*? I wondered.

We walked around the entire building. There didn't seem to be any way the mummy mover could get in.

"Ashley, look at that window," I said, pointing a few feet above our heads. I can see some familiar-looking paintings on the wall inside."

"The mummy room!" she said. "I'll boost you up and you can look inside. See if the mummy is still there."

Ashley cupped her hands together. I stepped into them. "Don't fall!" she said. "Okay. One, two...three! Here goes!"

With a grunt, Ashley hoisted me up to the window. I grabbed onto the sill and peered inside.

"Oh, no!" I groaned.

"What's wrong?" Ashley asked.

"I can see into the sarcophagus," I told her. "The mummy is gone again."

"Are you sure?" Ashley called up to me.

"Yes—" I started to say. "Whoa! Ohhhhh!

Ahhh!" I lost my balance and tried to grab on to the windowsill.

"Hold on!" Ashley cried.

It was too late. I wobbled...and wobbled some more. Ashley stepped around to keep up with me. But then I wobbled all the way to the left and fell—right on top of Ashley.

We landed in a heap in a bush under the window.

"Are you all right?" she asked.

"I think so," I said.

"What's that on your jacket?" Ashley pointed to a big grease stain on my sleeve.

"I don't know. I wonder where it came from," I said.

"There!" Ashley shouted, pointing to the wall behind the bush.

We saw a large round opening in the wall. It was covered with a metal grate, stained with black grease. The grate was hanging halfway off the wall.

"This is it!" I cried. "This must be how the

mummy mover is getting into the museum!"

"Let's check it out!" Ashley said.

Ashley and I grabbed the grate and pulled. It came off easily in our hands—and left grease on our fingers.

"Yuck! This stuff is sticky," I said, wiping my hands on my jacket.

We peered into the hole—into a dark tunnel about three feet across.

The tunnel was probably an old air vent. It looked really creepy. But we had to check it out—and see where it led.

I crept inside. Ashley followed behind me. We crawled and crawled and crawled until we came to the end of the tunnel.

"There's another grate here!" I told Ashley.

"Okay," she said. "Try to push it off."

I pushed the grate. It moved a little. I tried again, but it was too heavy for me to move by myself.

"Ashley, grab the other side," I said. "I think two people have to push this thing."

Ashley squeezed in next to me. "Okay, one…two…three—push!" I said.

We did it! The grate fell to the floor of the museum with a heavy clang.

We jumped out of the tunnel. We were standing behind a suit of armor.

We grinned and gave each other a high five.

A few feet in front of us was the entrance to the mummy room!

13

NABBED!

The next morning, Ashley and I pedaled like crazy to get to school.

"I can't wait to tell everyone that we found out how the mummy mover has been getting into the museum!" Ashley said. "Now they'll have to believe the mummy isn't moving by itself."

"And I can't wait to see Patty's face when she knows we were right and she was wrong about the mummy's curse!" I said.

We raced into the school and down the hall

to our classroom.

Mr. Weitzberg and all the kids in our class were crowded around Fuzzball's cage.

"What happened?" I asked.

"Fuzzball's gone," Tim said sadly.

Patty scowled at us. "See? I told you our guinea pig would be next. Do you finally believe that we're cursed?"

Uh-oh. Suddenly I didn't feel so excited anymore. Ashley and I had figured out how the mummy mover was getting into the museum—but not *who* the mummy mover was! Or who did all those things to our class. We still had no idea who took Bun-Bun—and now Fuzzball!

Peter ran into the room. "Sorry I'm late," he panted as he unzipped his jacket. "I missed my bus."

I glanced at Peter—and gasped.

"I'm not *that* late, Mary-Kate," Peter said, laughing.

I looked over at Ashley. She was staring at

Peter, too—with her mouth wide open.

"Why are you two looking at me like that?" Peter asked nervously.

I pointed at him. "You're the one who's been moving the mummy!"

"You're crazy," Patty said.

"We can prove it," I said. I grabbed my backpack and pulled out my grease-stained jacket.

I pointed to Peter's jacket. On the sleeve was a big grease stain—exactly like mine!

"What's going on?" Patty demanded, scratching her neck. "What's the big deal about your dirty jackets?"

"Peter," I said, "where did you get that black stain on your jacket?"

"I...uh...I..." Peter stammered. His cheeks turned bright red.

"Hey!" Samantha said, staring at Peter's jacket. "It looks just like the kind of stain on Mary-Kate's jacket."

"It *is* the same kind of stain," I said. "And I

got mine when Ashley and I found out how the mummy mover has been sneaking into the museum."

"What are you talking about?" Patty demanded.

Ashley explained about the metal grate and the tunnel into the museum.

Everyone turned to Peter. He hung his head, but he didn't say anything.

"Ashley!" I exclaimed. "I think I just figured out what we've been missing all along! Peter, there is no way you could have pushed that grate off by yourself," I said. "It took two of us to do it."

"You're right," he said. "I was helping Bobby. He couldn't move the grate—or the mummy—with a broken arm."

Bobby! We ruled him out as a suspect because of his broken arm!

"Oh, I get it!" Ashley cried. "We should never have taken Bobby's name off our list of suspects! He wanted more people to visit the

mummy. That way he wouldn't lose his job."

"But he couldn't move the mummy without Peter's help!" I added. Now I understood everything.

"Peter?" Mr. Weitzberg asked. "Is this true?"

Peter looked miserable. "Yes. It's true."

"Did you hide our smocks?" Samantha asked. "And put the snakes in Mary-Kate and Ashley's desks? Did you take Bun-Bun and Fuzzball?

"Yes," Peter admitted.

"But why?" Sam asked.

"Yeah," Patty said angrily. "Why?"

"I wanted to make the curse look real," Peter explained.

"Why didn't you take my smock?" Patty asked.

"You didn't touch the scarab. So it made sense that your smock would still be there."

"Where are Bun-Bun and Fuzzball?" I asked.

"They're safe at my house. I'll bring them

back to school tomorrow. The smocks, too."

"Peter," Mr. Weitzberg said, "you'll have to tell Ms. Pemberly the truth. You know that, right?"

"I know," he said. "I caused her—and everyone else—a whole lot of trouble. I'm really sorry. Bobby and I will talk to Ms. Pemberly after school. We'll tell her everything."

"Okay," Mr. Weitzberg said. "Everyone back to your desks."

"Well, I guess you were right about the mummy, after all," Patty said. "It wasn't cursed. But that means I was right, too."

"Right about what?" Ashley asked.

"Mummies are *bor-ing*!" she snickered.

As we took our seats, Peter tapped me on the shoulder. "Will you both come with me to the museum after school to talk to Ms. Pemberly?" he asked.

"Sure," I said. "You know, there is one good thing that came out of all this."

"What?" Peter asked.

"We now have two new smocks for painting!" I said, pointing to our ruined jackets.

We all laughed.

Ashley and I gave each other another high five.

The Trenchcoat Twins had cracked another case!

14

ALL WRAPPED UP!

"...And that's how we moved the mummy," Peter told Ms. Pemberly.

It was after school, and Ashley and I stood in the mummy room with Ms. Pemberly, Bobby, and Peter.

"I'm really sorry, Ms. Pemberly," Bobby said. "I know what my brother and I did was wrong. It's all my fault. I'm the one who asked Peter to help me move the mummy. I didn't want the Egyptian wing to close."

Ms. Pemberly looked at him sternly. "I

understand how you feel, Bobby. I appreciate how much you like working here in the Egyptian wing. And I think I can still trust you to be an honest worker. But I can't let everyone go on believing the mummy mysteriously moves by itself."

Bobby hung his head.

"I have a great idea," a man's voice said.

We all turned around to see Joe Marshall standing in the doorway, smiling.

"Who says you have to tell anyone anything?" he asked.

"What do you mean?" Ms. Pemberly replied.

"*How* the mummy was moving can be our secret," Mr. Marshall said. "Now that you've hired me back, no one will expect the mummy to move again. Because I'll be there watching that mummy all through the night!"

"You're right!" Ms. Pemberly told Mr. Marshall.

Then she turned to Ashley and me. "After the mummy moved again last night, I asked

Mr. Marshall to take his job back. He's much better than an alarm system any day!" She smiled. "And I want to thank you. We couldn't have solved this case without the Olsen and Olsen Mystery Agency."

"Well," Ms. Pemberly," I said, grinning. "I guess the case of the missing mummy is all wrapped up!"

Hi from the both of us,

Ashley and I couldn't wait to visit Great-grandma Olive. Great-grandma Olive is the best detective around. We learned everything we know about detective work from her.

When we got to Grandma's, we had a big surprise. Someone broke into her detective clubhouse. And all the suspects were—detectives!

Our next surprise was when Great-grandma Olive asked us to help solve the case!

But our biggest surprise was the giant footsteps we discovered on the dining room ceiling. Giant footsteps—made by a giant rabbit! What was going on here?

And what about the strange message we found: The Dragon Sings at Dawn. What did that mean?

We didn't have a lot of answers, but we did know one thing--this was going to be our weirdest case ever!

Want to find out some more? Take a look at the sneak peek on the next page for The New Adventures of Mary-Kate & Ashley: The Case Of The Surprise Call.

See you next time!

Love

Mary-Kate and Ashley

The New Adventures of
MARY-KATE & ASHLEY

A sneak peek at our next mystery...

The Case Of The
SURPRISE CALL

THUNK-THUNK!

"I hear footsteps!" I said to Ashley.

"I hear them, too," she said. "Heavy footsteps! Someone's downstairs!"

THUNK-THUNK! THUNK-THUNK!

"But we're the only ones in the detective clubhouse!" I whispered.

"Not anymore!" Ashley said. "We have to see who's down there!"

We tiptoed down the stairs of Great-grandma Olive's detective clubhouse. I listened for the footsteps. But the clubhouse was silent now.

"Which way should we go?" I asked, staring up and down the long hall.

“I don’t know,” Ashley whispered. “I’ll go left. You go right.”

I crept down the hall to the first door. I pressed my ear against it. I didn’t hear anything.

I opened it a crack and peered inside. No one was there.

One door down. About a million to go, I thought. This clubhouse is huge!

I inched my way over to the next door. I reached for the doorknob.

“Mary-Kate!” Ashley shouted from the dining room. “You’re not going to believe what I found! Come quick!”

I raced into the room—and saw Ashley staring at footprints on the floor.

Enormous footprints!

Each one was bigger than my head!

“What could have made these?” Ashley asked, staring at them.

“Some kind of animal,” I answered. “A *giant* animal!”

I bent down to get a closer look. Each footprint was divided into round sections. Sort of like the pads on the bottom of a dog's paw.

I stood up and followed the trail of footprints across the floor.

"Um, Ashley," I gulped. "Look where the footprints go!"

Ashley's glance followed the footprints as they continued up the wall—and straight across the ceiling!

"This doesn't make any sense!" I said. "What kind of animal can walk on the ceiling?"

"I don't know," Ashley said, "But I'll bet there's a book on animal tracks in the library. I'll go upstairs and look. I'll be right back."

"Be careful," I said. "Whatever made these tracks might still be in the clubhouse."

Ashley ran up the stairs and came back with a book.

We flipped through the pages, looking back and forth from the drawings in the book to the huge tracks.

"The footprints are about as big as elephant tracks," Ashley said. "But they don't look like elephant tracks at all."

"Keep going," I said.

"They don't match tiger tracks. Or wolf tracks. Or any kind of bird tracks," she said. "And they don't match gorilla tracks. Or deer tracks. Or armadillo tracks."

Ashley turned another page in the book.

"That's it!" I exclaimed, staring at the page. "That's a match!"

"But it can't be," Ashley said, frowning. She studied the page.

"Why?" I asked. "What animal is that?"

"It's a bunny!" she said.

A bunny? I thought. How could a bunny have made these giant footprints? Or walked up the wall and across the ceiling?

"The only bunny that could have made these footprints is a *giant* bunny." I shook my head, confused.

"Yeah," Ashley answered. She glanced at

the footprints on the ceiling. "A giant flying bunny."

Singing dragons, surprise calls from mysterious strangers, and giant flying bunnies. This was turning out to be our strangest case ever!

Mary-Kate & Ashley's Cassettes and CDs
Available Now Wherever Music is Sold

Lightyear Entertainment

DUALSTAR RECORDS

Distributed in the U.S. by wea